Lord, YOU SUPPLY

I0526699

Recipe :

A Love to Write!

Every story ever told has a beginning
and an end.
From the moment I realized, it is your
goodness and mercy I live to
comprehend!
I rely on the simple reflections, to get
me to the next level in peace.
A forth coming of a charismatic
redemption, to reach my full potential,
in time to release.
I press deeper and deeper towards the
mark of the High calling, without
hesitation.
A humbled sacrifice, equipped to write
encouraging poems, sending healing to
a wounded nation.

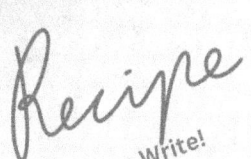

THE MAIN Ingredients...

RAVEN CHASITY ROGERS

Lord, You Supply The Main Ingredients...

Raven Chasity Rogers

If you purchased this book without a cover, you should be aware that this book is stolen property. It was reported as "unsold and destroyed" to the publisher, and the author has not received payment for this "stripped book."

ISBN Number: 0-9960743-9-1 (Paperback)

ISBN Number: 0-9960743-8-4 (E-Book)

LCC Number: 2024908022

Lord, You Supply The Main Ingredients...

Copyright © 2024 Raven Chasity Rogers

Edited by Cynthia M. Portalatín

Published by:

PO Box 1819, Owings Mills, MD 21117

www.maynetre.com

All rights reserved. Except for use in the case of brief quotations embodied in critical articles and reviews, the reproduction or utilization of this work in whole or part in any form by any electronic, digital, mechanical, or other means, now known or hereafter invented, including xerography, photocopying, scanning, recording, or any information storage or retrieval system, is forbidden without written prior permission of the author and publisher, Maynetre Manuscripts, LLC.

The scanning, uploading, and distribution of this book via the Internet or via any other means without permission of the publisher and author is illegal and punishable by law. Purchase only authorized versions of this book, and do not participate in or encourage electronic piracy of copyrighted materials. Your support of the author's rights is appreciated.

Printed in the United States of America

First Printing 2024

10 9 8 7 6 5 4 3 2 1

✾ Created with Vellum

Dedication

This third book is dedicated to The Ultimate Powers that be! Yes, I said it! The Holy Trinity! For showing me that anything is possible when you follow after righteousness and seek God first!

Table of Contents

Section III: A Touch of Strength!!!

Foreword

Tremayne Moore

I have had the privilege and honor to watch Raven write over 100 poems over a span of one-to-two years, and they capture the heart and mind of God. I stand in amazement, as she is about to release this third book within the span of 12 months. If you haven't realized by now, Raven has a writing gift, and she has something to say for those who have an ear. As you enter this book, **Lord, You Supply The Main Ingredients...**, you are about to experience the love of God through its pages. So, get comfortable and open your heart to the writing of Raven Chasity Rogers.

Section I: A Touch of God!!!

Lord, You Supply the Main Ingredients
4/5/2023

God, no other ingredient equals the amount of impeccable goodness, coming from You.
The bread of Life, Your unfailing Love, and Holy Spirit are so powerful to equip me through.
In prayer, by faith I enter humbly, seeking Your Holy presence in the secret place.
By Your Spirit, I am delivered with Your special touch, authority, mercy, and grace!
Lord, You supply A Strawberry Kind of Love, to look past my faults and see my needs.
As I enjoy Your marvelous wonders, pouring out Raspberry Blessings as You take the lead.
Emblazon Your light to the paths ahead by shining a Lemon-Filled Son-Rise, guiding me all the way.
Overjoyed with holiness, filled with Your truth and a Slice of Orange Happiness, You are forever here to stay.

God, the Honorable!

5/27/2023

Again, I say, Greater is the One who dwells on the inside of me, than the irrelevant one in the world.
I present to You out of a cheerful heart, because
I am that grateful girl!
You enable your Son to cause my light to shine, and
ALL of the credit goes to You!
Because the breath of life, feels good throughout, sending praises up to Heaven, is what I do!
Cover my visions and dreams from the corruptive naysayers, trying to creep in unaware; so they tarry.
Chaperone over the harvest that is waiting for me to gather graciously, without me being weary!
God, You are worth every mention! It is impossible to complete with anyone else, and that's why I come to know, Your love for me shows clearly!

A Follow-Through God!
5/6/2023

Identified in the scriptures as the Alpha and the Omega, the beginning and the end.
Untouchable, I am, to the chaos that is around me. A divine blessing You will send!
I give You permission to search my heart, scraping off all unwanted fragments left behind.
You have blessed the Awakened Dreams to follow through when creative ideas come to mind.
I can count on Your every word coming to pass, because You Are My Real Promise!
It is my faith in You, although the blessings are not yet visible, the evidence is bliss!
Don't do it! Life is too precious to take part in a Sour Masquerade.
His pure, red blood shed on the cross is a manifestation, that I'm a Sure Overcomer, He made!
Because I have been saved by a God who will always follow through.

Abundantly, this Chocolate Covered Miracle is destined and hand selected to be used, by You!

My Splendid Carpenter
5/5/2023

God, You are the absolute best to ever do it!
Using mighty power to craft me back together has not been a
challenge for You.
There are only great results, when You perform, nothing
remains untrue.
Whenever my life seems out of place, a touch of Your grace
places me back together.
Too splendid in All of Your ways! I'm pressed, but in due time
all things are made better!
Lord, you are the only right friend I have, who erases every act
of my wrong doing.
I experience the ability of Your workmanship on my behalf,
because I trust and keep moving!
Shape me for the good, Holy Spirit! I can't do it without Your
direction, no matter how hard I try!
Please create a pure heart within me;
so, kind gestures are performed without that awkward sigh.
Graciously, polish me anew so all may see and it's to You they
will draw nigh!

Yes, God Did It Right!!!
5/15/2023

Stampede over all seen and unseen warfare, please, throughout the night!
Sanitize my mind fully in Your word, to overcome this fight!
Sacred are Your ways to help me live right!
Surround me around loving people; now, that is real tight!
Set my eyes upon You daily; grant me with spiritual insight!
Surely, Your paths are made clear, 'cause You are my light!
Sever the hand of the enemy, with Your power and Your might!
Submitting to Your will! Allow my life to take flight!
Sowing seeds of His goodness within me, for a harvest delight!
Surrender all my cares directly to You, so I don't need to be uptight!
Spotting my inconsistencies, forgive me, Lord! There's a new spark to ignite!
Searching my heart leaving no room, for evil words to recite!
Subtitles to the words of Your songs, singing praises forever! It's alright!
Shouting loud in triumphant victories, more and more, make room for love; lets unite!

It is God! Just Like That!
5/27/2023

Every moment should be appreciated with thanksgiving. Your wise instructions will make it plain!
Obedience is the key to fulfillment! Reminding us that our "labour is not in vain!"
Search the scriptures and you will find the true and loving One, Jehovah-Jireh; He will supply!
Don't get discouraged! Trust in Him along the way and allow the doubters to walk on by!
Every moment calls for a celebration. Enjoy the present! Don't take it for granted!
And watch the One from whom all blessings flow, water you with new life, wherever you are planted!

You Are My Real Promise
4/7/2023

Since then, I wondered, why? How could You speak such a prophetic melody over me, when I didn't walk in Your way?
In fact, it was Your love that looked beyond my fault, quite noticeable on that wooden cross for display!
You protect me from the false narratives, of the doubters, whose actions hold no type of weight.
Every outcome works out beautifully, no matter what the state!
A realm of remarkability, show me as my heart is curious to explore!
Because my soul yearns for Your effervescent purpose, to saturate me more and more!
Absorbing from that moment, a major covenant keeper. You're the real blessing! I receive!
Your every word spoken over my destiny, an orchestrated harmony, I believe!
A dissertation proven factually, no one can take away Your truth planted in me.
As long as I stand firm on Your solid foundation, my special rock, You remain to be!

Significant Compassion
4/26/2023

A solved mystery, without the need for a search, has been gifted
to us so obviously!
The importance of His full compassion poured out upon us, to
be shared throughout, willingly!
Lord, you don't have to take anything back! A true example for
the faint of heart, and the broken one.
There is still much to learn about Your everlasting love
that draws me closer and closer to your Son!
The greeting is so majestic! Everything about Him captivates
the essence of my whole entire being!
Genuinely, laid out for me to model, yet I stand to live a beautiful life, worth seeing!
Your real sentiments come from a place some have waited their
whole life just to feel.
To be treated with significant compassion, a deep experience of
excitement, indeed, to know it's all real!

Beautified F.A.I.T.H.
5/20/2021

FOREVER and ever, I will believe, even when the blessing is not yet tangible!

AWARDED by God, the Perfect One, because I realize and trust, that He is surely able!

IN agreement with His purpose for my life, despite the vicissitudes, He will dismantle!

THE Only Supernatural being throughout the universe, who illuminates my life to shine bright!

HIGHEST in regards giving all Honor due; accepting everything about Him is extremely right!

The Right Forfeit
5/29/2023

All I desire to do is praise You, please You and live faithful no matter the circumstances.

Forfeiting and leaving behind the very unlawful things, while leaving no ounce of space for consequences.

Please water me daily, and nurture me to be rooted and fruitful in You, showing off with different dances.

In the meantime, I am handing every insignificant issue over to You so I can seize each and every moment of these great and marvelous chances!

I Am the Beautiful!
6/1/2023

It becomes a mandate for me, during this time, to appreciate life more and not settle for less!
I am the beautiful elegance flowing through the fabric of a captivating and whimsical dress!
I am the beautiful presence changing atmospheres in the room, because I am not here for the mess!
I am the beautiful painting on the canvas, a special piece, a true work of art!
I am the beautiful writer sharing my gift with an audience, as I reveal what's on my heart!
I am the beautiful creation secretly hidden, not yet discovered, but one of a kind!
I am the beautiful flower blooming in its season, a great asset, yet rare to find!
I am the beautiful radiance to brighten up your day, giving you the strength to keep going!
I am the beautiful spirit filled with a purpose, looking up to the Highest, to keep on flowing!

Truly B.L.E.S.S.E.D.
5/17/2023

BELIEVING the possibilities with the beauty of pure light!
LOVE is the foundation of it all, selfless and shown, both day and night!
EXISTS more and more, open up and smile again! Let it reach out and soar!
SO it remains, while growing strong, making room to explore!
SOMEONE out there is waiting for a sign to stand up and feel alive!
EMBRACES a new hope and chapter written well, to keep it moving, rise and strive!
DESTINY obtaining to live out the masterpiece originally created. Lean forward and take a dive!

A Love to Write!
6/1/2023

Every story ever told has a beginning and an end.
From the moment I realized, it is your goodness and mercy I
live to comprehend!
I rely on the simple reflections, to get me to the next level in
peace.
A forth coming of a charismatic redemption, to reach my full
potential, in time to release.
I press deeper and deeper towards the mark of the High calling,
without hesitation.
A humbled sacrifice, equipped to write encouraging poems,
sending healing to a wounded nation.

And Here It Is!
6/1/2023

A dash of love, a sprinkle of hope, with an ounce of kindness is
here to stay!
120 poems written. Who's keeping count? Without God, what
is there left to say?
His favor reigns down, 'cause I am unique! His generosity
towards me is Heavenly greeted!
A made-up mind, picked from a meadow of flowers, a life by
design, can't be repeated!
From His wonderful capabilities, He grants me the satisfaction
in this lifetime to obtain!
That the work I do for Him will last, and His presence ever-
lasting will always remain!

God, a True Story!
5/29/2023

In the past, You have helped me to grow up by exposing the worst of my tantrums.

The necessary correction of my actions were lessons learned, which granted me a life of better outcomes.

So, be the driving force on this pathway, as You open my eyes to meaningful discoveries.

Settle my heartbeats with a pleasant rhythm from the spoken word of your triumphant love stories.

Pronounced from the kingdom of Your dear Son, I bask in peace, giving You all of the glory!

Never sever the sacraments bringing us together, provided by Your Word and my powerful testimony!

Reflection

1. Who do you think each poem within the section "A Touch of God" is written to?

2. What comes to mind as you read each poem in this section?

3. What's your favorite line(s) in each poem within this section?

4. If you had to add another stanza to each poem within this section, what would you write?

Section II: A Touch of Fruit!!!

A Strawberry Kind of Love
4/4/2023

Red and lovely in color, so wonderful and pleasing to the eyes.
A vivacious resemblance of a delightful time,
withdrawing positive and good vibes!
Your love is sweet to the taste and a beautiful depiction to my
soul, altogether bold!
A symbolic expression of the red blood, so precious to fulfill
one's life ever told.
Mighty is the meaning of what You display, because You're
greater than anything!
And to top it off, Your great Spirit resides in every born-again,
spiritual being!
You enrich even the greatness of creation, while forgiving every
ounce of wrongdoing we've ever done.
Every sin attached itself to the Love You sacrificed for us, while
beaming in the sun.
Giving a significant contribution to our overall, spiritual self
and well-being.
Oh how excellent! Yes, excellent!
That You're the greatest love in the world worth seeing!

Blueberry Skies
4/4/2023

Way up high in the sky dwells the blueness of Your artistry, where the clouds and the birds occupy.

Even the attendance of the wildlife they stop and stare, while their eyes gaze upon the pretty blue sky.

So rich in its presentation, an immaculate view, that it offers to us, makes due.

Maintaining clear skies in the morning, and throughout the day, speaks volumes about You!

Everything You represent is incredible! You are a great source for the body inside and out!

And to make mention, a loving peace to our mental health and reassurance; that's what it's all about!

Projecting from on high, there's enough from You to go around, for all to see passing by.

Smiling down so Heavenly, from the awakening of the tenacious Blueberry clear sky!

Lemon-Filled Son-Rise
4/4/2023

I love how Your glory shines down with compassion, filling up
the atmosphere.
A marvelous God all around, showing us that You are always
right there!
You rise early in the morning, subjecting
the dawning of a new day.
Sitting high, shining bright on assignment, You wouldn't have it
any other way.
A citrus scent coming from the huge lemon tree planted
nearby.
Growing tall, being fed by the sunlight,
it's captivating! Oh my!
Not willing to escape the purpose and an opportunity to plant
that great seed!
The provision of the Son-rise is the guiding light to the truth,
that we'll forever need!

An Orange Slice of Happiness
4/4/2023

Another gift so graciously given the ability to open in the morning is my beautiful sight
Everything about the quality of its use just leaves me feeling so right.
Receiving a jumpstart to a brand new and a gorgeous day!
Feels like an Orange Slice of Happiness, to a favorite song playing on replay.
Peeling back and seeing the delicious slices of the orange, fitly joined together.
A specialty to the citrus goodness inside,
making everything that much better!
As it relates to life, every bit of it is a refreshing piece of a promise, from all the madness.
That enables us to enjoy every day so pleasantly with a slice of gladness!

Raspberry Blessings!
4/4/2023

Too sweet, adorable, delicate, and unique with a smooth sensation on my heart.
A cluster of blessings after blessings,
what a great way to start!
This unusual kind of fruit reminds me of the sweetness of Your true love that I adore!
Formulating an example of an open Heaven, full of great treasures and more!
Radically, shower down on me tasty blessings, showing off, for all to stare!
In amazement, Lord, You're the answer to my prayers and the real reason why I'm here!
With a sincere amount of gratitude, I am ready to receive!
The fruitfulness of my harvest, it's time to reap, because I truly believe!

Chocolate Covered Miracles
4/10/2023

The impact will set off alarms, an explosive banger of
expansion!
Holy Spirit opening Supernatural doors, catapulting me to
another dimension!
Visual effects seen of His gentleness and mercies to help every-
thing just settle in.
The beginning of the most breathtaking life story, a new
chapter written. Here's how it will begin!
Tried by the fire, smoking hot! Can't you see that I am the apple
of His eye?
Rebuking the devourer for my sake, demolishing demons! So
long, you had your try!
Who would have imagined, a gentle morsel, birthed from my
mother's precious womb?
Adopted into His kingdom empire, before Jesus was ever laid
up in the tomb.
It is the marvel of His glory and righteousness, a true love story,
that abounds!

Lord, You Supply The Main Ingredients...

Everything I've been waiting for, I search in Him, a miracle
worker, I have found!
On that note, a caption recognized and fit for the Master's use,
He covers me all around!

A Smooth-Like-Butter Transition

4/10/2023

I beseech you all, let's incorporate, have a
fun time and get it in!
Spreading Agape love and good tidings so pleasantly,
It will always win!
Our imperfections, stirred to perfection with a touch of grace,
to walk in that marvelous light!
A smooth transition, rich and creamy like butter, simply great!
It is out of sight!
To embrace what the Lord has done for us; when He says,
you're ready! Arise and move!
It's a transition so necessary, with the right ingredients added
for your good! Yet tangible!
Let me just set this reminder here. It was NEVER about us,
from the very beginning.
Because it was His Son, who paid the price! I don't hear you,
now, what are you saying?
His pure blood runs deeply through our veins, all who believe
and receive! We walk by faith, no need to see!

Lord, You Supply The Main Ingredients...

Hold on and trust Him with an understanding that, one day,
we'll reign with Jesus, so
Heavenly!

Watermelon Wisdom
5/8/2023

Planted within the ground, waiting for a beautiful harvest to
take root.
Powerful seeds nestled inside the skin of such a popular fruit.
Lord, just like the watermelon is attached to the vine, keep me
connected to you, with wisdom.
For it is the principal thing that will help guide me, to stand
upright, while tasting freedom!

I strive to grow in Your grace, and to be wise enough to walk
away from evil conflict.
It's a delight from this watery fruit, a refreshment to admire. So,
I thirst for Your knowledge to be wit!

What a loving outcome it will be, to know waiting patiently
can't offset me from growing.
The benefits of your wise counsel and knowledge, I grab hold,
to release the beautiful seeds I am sowing!

It Is So, and Too Sweet!
5/19/2023

A sweet-smelling Savior, your aroma flowing freely with new mercies, in the morning time.

Keep my mind filled with creativity and my heart overflowing to write dope poetry, that rhymes!

A sincere congratulations Lord, for supplying the main ingredient in me, to put out this great, blessed work!

Every time someone reads the words of your goodness, let a willingness to receive You be on high alert!

With no restrictions, I hold on to the sweetness of your wisdom, springing instructions from the ground!

Let the words of my mouth, and meditation of my heart, be acceptable in your sight, with protection all around.

Send harmonious sound waves of Your power throughout, making your Heavenly presence known!

You cause my behavior to become frolic, as I acknowledge Your smile upon me from the throne.

Feed my hunger with the life of Your bread, and bid me to drink from Your Spirit, when I thirst!

33

Too sweet to know, marked by the Prolific One, who sealed the deal, when He created me to always keep Him first!

A Sweet Resignation
4/17/2023

It is with great joy and extreme happiness, to share, with
respect, my remarks on today!
Yeah, indeed! A tasteful surprise to this great announcement!
Let me be abrupt and just say!
Two weeks for a heads up is unnecessary, to say the least, in
this case.
The signs to move on and do something new are reading real
clear on my face.
A sweet escape to what I envision! True possibilities are always
near!
Instantly, rejoicing in faith all around, dismissing every doubt
and the fear.
I'm so prepared to get going; so, I can taste and see His good-
ness on arrival, for me!
Goodbye and thanks for the opportunity, now serving its
purpose as a piece of sweet history!

Reflection

1. Who do you think each poem within the section "A Touch of Fruit" is written to?

2. What comes to mind as you read each poem in this section?

3. What's your favorite line(s) in each poem within this section?

4. If you had to add another stanza to each poem within this section, what would you write?

Section III: A Touch of Strength!!!

Awakened Dreams!
4/10/2023

Awaken now! Arise up, from the settle of your rest!
Destiny is waiting to be fulfilled. Let's go without resistance!
You are next!
Get away from the busyness of the distracting things in life you
can't control!
Submit and allow the delightfulness of your awakened dreams
to be that ever-changing goal!
Prepare, in a state of celebration, to see them all
come to a quick reality!
Reignite the passion from within, to be spoken with an under-
standing and a true certainty.
No more will you embezzle the awakening of your dreams,
again to be postponed!
Instead, give way to the declarations out loud, from an outra-
geous pressure ever to be groaned!
The isolation so gratuitous is no longer welcomed. Please, hear
me out!
Begin to live out your awakened dreams, in faith. See them
manifest before you, without a doubt!

Untouchable, I Am
4/2/2023

Touched by His Mighty hand, untouchable to man, that I Am!
Anointed and chosen since birth, raised to show respect. Yes,
sir and yes, ma'am!
He rebukes the devourer for my sake, even though I made so
many mistakes.
Overshadowed by Him, the enemy has to get His permission to
come my way.
Grateful, 'cause the Greater One lives inside of me from day-to-
day.
Really terrific! You enable me to draw close, and it's in You I
abide!
Thank you for a power truly electric! Permitting every dark
force to flee on every side.
Gladly, I am surrounded and shielded by Your loving grace.
Your hedge of protection, restricts my enemies from coming
anywhere near my face.
Superb are Your ways!
Granting me the favor to succeed!

Lord, You Supply The Main Ingredients...

And an understanding to hear and do
everything to always stay freed!

Polished Diamond
12/1/2022

Shaped symmetrically, captivating, and glossy to a perfection, completely distinguished!
Righteous and lively! You shine richly, and the outcome is an astonishment to be relinquished!
The arrangement of Your ways share a beautiful tale, without taking away from its reflection!
I long to appreciate the quality and solid form that characterizes Your subjection!
Worthy to be counted, simply because, who You are is genuine alongside other fine-cut, pretty diamonds!
You don't fit in amongst the ones that come across rushed and shaped like almonds!
A true presentation standing out, next to the fake, that's what it takes to seal the prize!
A high-market value you possess, because Your worth rises high, deleting every hidden disguise!
A statement piece some may mimic, You pose a threat, too official and overall the realest thing!

Lord, You Supply The Main Ingredients...

Always stay true, 'cause only what's real will shine without a need for all of the extra bling!

A Sure Overcomer!
4/19/2023

Sit back and watch me soar over your head, like an eagle!
Patiently waiting to take off and fly high.
Now, watch what God do!
Prospering like never before! So, please excuse you!
A testament calling on my life, too gracious and true!
Flowing in the Holy Spirit, speaking the real truth!
Glorifying the Highest of High! His praise
surpassing the roof!
Adjust your attitude, because all of His real
love is just remarkable!
Shutting the mouths of naysayers, who talk trash, but they have
no clue!
It's okay! You are forgiven! Please take a breath,
before you turn blue!
A for-sure season, don't give up and wait! Your
turn will come to you!
Meditate on His word, both day and night, and
watch Him follow through!

Lord, You Supply The Main Ingredients...

Overall, don't panic! Everything is alright!
We win!
He's always there for you!

To Be Continued... With Thanks
4/10/2023

Truthfully, from the utmost and beginning of time, You've
always had the first and final say.
Breathing life and making all things come about, handling busi-
ness without dismay.
Written off by the best and worst of them, only You can turn it
all around!
To be continued with thanks to You, a loving Savior, in me, you
will surround!
The awful feelings of hopelessness left me secluded and igno-
rant of Your perfect sacrifice.
Applying pressure to be free, instantly, 'cause I want Your
forgiveness to suffice.
So effortlessly created, to be continued, to live, because of Your
kind and spoken word!
And just like that, my heart is opened wide, making room to
receive every promise so eloquently heard!
With thanks, You transform every part of my being, a joy to
move about purposefully!

Lord, You Supply The Main Ingredients...

A prize possession, depicted and dedicated with mercy, devotion, and sincerity!

And a respect to say thank You, for the encouragement and faith, that every promise will be fulfilled by You, successfully!

New Destiny For Me!
5/18/2023

Delegate Your passions unto me, as I move onward, in the fullness of my purpose!
Command Your Spirit to fall fresh on me, symbolizing I am worthy of this!
Absolutely, You redeem the time; so I walk steady by faith, with hope, and charity to endure the race.
Small glimpses of the future, He reveals in due time. Trust in God, with a shout, but I must pick up the pace!
A beloved sanctification by washing away the old and making plenty of room for the new.
Glory to You! I wouldn't have it any other way! So faithful, You are through and through!
A supply of newness all around, a change in my mindset is where to start!
As I take a step with the courage to believe, my life begins to unfold a blessed work of art!
Giving it my all and nothing less, I trust in Him as I draw nigh.
A destiny so new, You and I are never apart!

Hey! Who Cares What You Think About Me?

5/12/2023

Kudos! Much love, but it is not of my concern what you say or even think about me.

I must stand firm, head held high, growing in His grace and knowledge invariably!

Fearfully and wonderfully made is what the All-knowing One rightfully declares over me!

The lamp unto my feet, and light to my path, to walk in all of His ways spiritually!

Relying on the protection of my Holy Master, who provides it to me daily and mercifully!

Your thoughts do not matter and have no power over me. I am covered all around! I hope you see!

To remain a hearer and a doer of His word, to move about in this life, tenaciously!

Adios! It's a wrap! I humbly submit bowing down, to the royalty of His fulfilling majesty!

A Champion Mindset in Me!
5/29/2023

Mercifully, You'd cleanse the nature of my old thoughts, with a fresh and inclusive makeover.

Prepping for battles ahead, all of a sudden, a glimpse appears before me, winning in an epic takeover!

This championship already belongs to me, because you've given me strategies from the Master Playbook.

Drawing it out, with a play-by-play selection of what's to come, I have your favor on me, to get the first look.

Examples of David's, Joshua and Caleb's victories elate in me a reminder of how it is done!

A celebratory mindset of a champion is a guarantee that every act of faith is a VICTORY already won!

The Path Is Made Clear!
5/27/2023

Do not get stuck in the mundane of what used to be!
Everything that did not work out for you is now a part of
history.
Pat yourself on the back, and speak the word of God to yourself
out loud!
He will clear a path for you and set you apart from the unruly
crowd.
Lean not to your own understanding! You are covered when
you put on the whole armor of God!
To endure the journey set before you by the protection of His
mighty Shepherd's rod.

(Clothed) With Hope
5/23/2023

Father in You, nothing goes unnoticed and that's why my life does not remain the same.

The safest security, guarding my mind, soul, and body, from hope to everlasting, as I call upon Your name.

I must confess! There is so much to learn about You daily. I'm constantly doing research!

No one can figure You out! Your ways and thoughts are higher than the price of the best merch!

God, you are the holiest, flyest Creator and Educator on this planet, Earth!

I sit under Your tutelage, for an outpour; so, my hopes and dreams can come to pass by giving birth!

Continue to bless my mind and my hands, as You enhance the capabilities of my writing.

Disregarding the need to search elsewhere, Your truth matters the most, leaving me with hope, so inviting!

A Sour Masquerade!
4/21/2023

The presence of your bitter activity leaves an unforgettable
taste, quite drastically!
The sad arrogance of your development, in denial, running
from the truth, that's cowardly!
A facade putting on a great act, while speaking lies of deception
with your lips.
Robbing from the strength of those who care for you, a burden
for the weakest of fellowships.
A prime example to be held accountable, portraying the victim
every time.
You are a sour masquerade to every lie and, without a doubt, no
true friend of mine!

A Touch of Don't!
6/1/2023

Don't bow out or fearfully cave in! There is a means to an end!
Eventually, things will get better! This is as real as it gets! You
don't have to pretend!
If you need to start all over, it is okay! Take a nice, deep breath
and plow through it!
And watch the pieces to the puzzle, smoothly come together,
adjusting to the perfect fit!

A Touch of Faith!
6/1/2023

God used trailblazers in the Bible, to show us the rewards of their belief.

They chose to walk in paths they couldn't see, to trust in God was their relief!

Even though the direction of God seemed impossible, they kept on moving without a doubt!

Having faith the size of a mustard seed was all they needed for God to bring them out!

Moving mountains, conquering new territories, eating the good of the land, and much, much more!

I am astonished to bear witness that putting your total faith in God, no matter the loss, He will intentionally restore!

Your Power, You Supply!
5/27/2023

When the Spirit of God places something on your heart, get on the move; be boisterous, and simply stay lit!
This is the time; so, it can happen! It's not about you! It's all about Him. Now, let Him prove it!
No excuses! Stay the course, because the battle is a fixed fight! Indeed, you've already prophetically won!
A dynamic explosion, a show for the masses of His Heavenly presence is sure to come!

Graceful Gratitude!!!

5/27/2023

While eliminating the worry for tomorrow, His love is provided
for me day-by-day.
I am ambitious to know His Word will come to pass. I just stay
faithful along the way!
Put the talent to the test. Invest the time, and be on the lookout
for the treasure!
What's in store for you, no one can deplete it! God has so much
more! Who could measure?
For instance, the assignment to manifest three poetry books in a
short amount of time – He don't play!
Seldomly, the happy tears falling from my eyes, leaves me taken
aback in the most amazing way!
I pray each poem aims towards your heart with a simple
message that you can take, and paints a gentle picture in your
mind, as if you were reading it comfortably by a quiet lake!
With gratitude, this delightful chapter must come to an end. A
new one awaits. Don't be sad! There are more memories
aligned for me to make!

Reflection

1. Who do you think each poem within the section "A Touch of Strength" is written to?

2. What comes to mind as you read each poem in this section?

3. What's your favorite line(s) in each poem within this section?

4. If you had to add another stanza to each poem within this section, what would you write?

Acknowledgments

Thank you, Heavenly Father, for the manifestation of this 3rd book and a sincere thanks for the great things to come!

Also, a special thank you to my Pops, Mr. Roy Rogers, for the genuine support and words of affirmation along the way! To all of my kinfolk, a lovingly thank you! An additional thank you to those who showed me support, whether past or present. A heart felt thank you to Maynetre Manuscripts, LLC, for the publishing of another dope book, and to his editor, Cynthia M. Portalatin, thanks a bunch!

Furthermore, to all of the support moving forward, a thanks of gratitude goes to you!

About the Author

Raven Chasity Rogers is a poet and author, who enjoys writing poetry by the grace of God. She hopes to encourage readers and bring smiles to their faces as they turn the pages. She is the author of *God Sent The Raven* and *Jesus (Holy Spirit) Is My Ghostwriter*. She claims that writing these poetry books has been incredible in many ways and opened up doors to new blessings.

www.ingramcontent.com/pod-product-compliance
Lightning Source LLC
Chambersburg PA
CBHW070829250626
47170CB00006B/2261